Monkey
and the Little One

For Mia and Molly

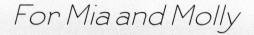

EGMONT

We bring stories to life

First published in Great Britain 2015 by Egmont UK Limited
This edition published 2018 by Dean,
an imprint of Egmont UK Limited,
The Yellow Building, 1 Nicholas Road, London, W11 4AN
www.egmont.co.uk

Text and illustration copyright © Claire Alexander 2015
Claire Alexander has asserted her moral rights.

ISBN 978 0 6035 7566 2

70166/001

Printed in Malaysia

A CIP catalogue record for this title is available from the British Library.

Stay safe online. Egmont is not responsible for content hosted by third parties.

Egmont takes its responsibility to the planet and its inhabitants very seriously.
All the papers we use are from well-managed forests run by responsible suppliers.

Monkey
and the Little One

Claire Alexander

Monkey lived all
alone in the jungle.

He liked it that way.

He enjoyed
eating bananas …

reading books . . .

and swimming in the cool blue lake.

But one day Monkey found he was no longer alone.

He didn't know why the Little One had come,
but he certainly didn't want his company.

"Please go away," said Monkey.

The Little One just stared at him.
He didn't understand monkey-speak.

The Little One started making himself at home – right underneath Monkey's hammock!

He followed Monkey everywhere
and copied everything he did.

Yuck!

"Please go away," sighed Monkey.
But the Little One would not go away.

And at bedtime, things got much worse.
There was a **noisy crackle**,
followed by some very **loud music**.

"Please turn that **Off!**"

Monkey shouted.

But the Little One didn't pay attention
and the music went on all night.

The next morning, tired Monkey found a quiet spot.

But the Little One soon found it too. He brought Monkey a jam sandwich and a beautiful red flower.

"Please leave me alone!" cried Monkey,
and he stomped off for a swim.

As he sank into the cool water,
Monkey said, "Peace at last."

But he spoke too soon –
the Little One had followed him to the lake!

"Leave me alone!"

shouted Monkey.

This time the Little One
seemed to understand
monkey-speak and he left.

Monkey was alone again.
It was just what he wanted.
But somehow it didn't feel
the same as before.

He couldn't be bothered to
read a book or swim in the lake.

The next morning Monkey noticed the Little One
had left behind his tiny pot of jam and loaf of bread.

"What will he eat?" Monkey worried.
"He doesn't like bananas."

Monkey had to find the
Little One straight away.

He looked everywhere,
even climbing the tallest
tree, but there was no
sign of the Little One.

Monkey flopped down in despair.
Then he noticed one of the Little One's
favourite flowers.

There was one place he hadn't looked — the field
with the beautiful red flowers.

Monkey ran
as fast as he could.
He didn't stop
until he reached
the field . . .

"I've **found** you!" cried Monkey.
"Please come back!"

The Little One gave Monkey a big hug . . .

and Monkey gave him a small jam sandwich.

And things went back to the way they were before. The Little One still followed Monkey everywhere . . .

but somehow Monkey didn't mind anymore.

And so, Monkey and the Little One
stayed together in the jungle,
because they **both** liked it that way.